The Bass Factory

Lane Walker

The Fishing Chronicles
www.lanewalkerbooks.com

ISBN 978-1-955657-10-5
For Worldwide Distribution
Printed in the U.S.A.

Published by Bakken Books
2021
www.lanewalker.com

For more books, check out:
www.lanewalkerbooks.com

This book is dedicated to teachers and educators, thanks for giving children hope! Keep smiling and being a hero to so many.

- 1 -

"You fellas really want to win this thing? If you're serious, then you need to find the Bass Factory," the old man whispered in a hushed tone.

I could tell he didn't want anyone else at the gas station to hear what he was saying.

"Bass Factory? What's that? It sounds like something out of a fairy tale," I replied.

"It's no fairy tale. There's a Bass Factory out there on Lake Somerville. You find that spot, I guarantee you boys will win the bass tournament," the old man declared. "The Bass Factory is a hidden gem that has massive largemouth bass—the kind that will put you over the top. The only problem you're going to have is keeping your lure in the water."

"Keeping your line in the water?" I quickly asked. *"Because you're catching so many fish, you can't keep your line in the water?"* I shook my head.

The old man chuckled cryptically.

"No, I mean the kind where ferocious alligators snatch your fish off the line before you have time to pull it in," the old man explained.

"Alligators?" I frowned.

"Lake Somerville is known for its big bass, but we also have some of the nastiest gators on the planet. They get fat off all the fish in the lake. They love to eat bass, especially the big ones. But if the bass can survive, they get huge! The biggest bass in the lake will be close to the gators, but no one wants to fish near them. They leave gators alone," said the old man.

He asked me again, "How bad do you want to win this tournament? Are you willing to risk it all by getting close enough to land a monster? Or are you going to let them gators scare you off?" He grinned at me and nodded.

I glanced at my partner. I could tell by the look on

his face he was second-guessing fishing with me on Lake Somerville. While I valued his feelings, I also knew that he wasn't out here for the same reason I was. I loved to fish—especially for bass. It was my passion. I could fish all day, every day. But not him. He was there only because he had to be.

We both knew it, and I resented him. He had everything a kid could want. But I was slowly realizing that being a superstar wasn't all it was cracked up to be. I found out he fought a lot of the same insecurities I did. The difference was, he was the superstar, and I wasn't. But sometimes there are lessons that even an all-American quarterback can learn on a bass boat.

Personally, being on the water is therapeutic; it's my happy place. As soon as I flip the bail on my reel, everything feels right in the world. Fishing helps clear my mind and soul. It's my perfect place—somewhere I can just be me. It's a place where you don't have to be six foot four and fast as a jackrabbit.

My partner didn't feel the same way. He didn't

value the calming, lapping sound of the waves hitting the side of the boat.

He was here for one reason, and it wasn't a good one.

I wasn't sure taking him as my partner that day was going to bring me any trophy. *Why did I let myself get involved with his mess?*

-2-

Texas is well-known for plenty of things, but make no mistake, nothing is bigger than high school football. If I said football was important, that would be one of the biggest understatements ever. Football is a way of life in Texas.

In the fall, people treat every Friday night like a major holiday. Most local businesses shut down, and townspeople head out to support their local teams. If you play football, then you're treated like royalty. If you are a star quarterback on the football team, you're the biggest celebrity in town.

It's crazy! Adults treat high school athletes like they're movie stars. The local restaurants hang up their pictures and frame their jerseys. Football players seldom have to pay for their food when they go out to eat because everything is taken care of—all because they can throw a pigskin or tackle an opposing player.

Don't get me wrong; I love the game of football. Unfortunately for me, the game doesn't love me. I stand about 5'6" and weigh 150 pounds. My dad would always tell me, "Sorry, son, but Rock Conrad isn't made for football." I run the 40-yard dash slower than most and can't even catch a cold. I played football, or should I say, was on the football team until eighth grade.

I quickly realized my future and passion was in a different sport—bass fishing. While it's not football, bass fishing is still pretty big in Texas.

I grew up like a lot of teens, hunting and fishing while exploring the thousands of lakes in Texas. But fishing and the outdoors are what really motivate and excite me. I started to compete in bass fishing tournaments in ninth grade when I joined my local high school bass fishing team. And I was good.

Many people think fishing is all about luck. That may be true for the beginner or the casual fisherman but not for the expert. Fishing is a true craft. Catching one isn't about luck—it's about skill and strategy.

I became a student of the game of bass fishing. I watched videos and read everything I could about fishing, lake depths, casting methods, bait choices, and anything else that would help me hone my skills on the bass boat.

I was ranked in the top ten in all of Texas' high school bass fishing circuits. My high school, Polk High, was considered one of the top schools in the state and competed yearly for the state championship.

This year was going to be my best one yet. I was a four-year letter winner and captain of the Polk High Bass Fishing team. I had come up only a couple ounces short last year from being named state champion.

I spent all summer working on my boat and gear, and going fishing, perfecting my craft even more with my fishing teammate and partner, Eddie Falco, for three years. We worked well as a team. Eddie was a master at finding good locations and casting. My strengths were recognizing weather patterns, identifying currents, and having a passion for fishing.

Our coach called us the Dynamic Duo because he often teased us that we reminded him of Batman and Robin.

We started the season officially on Saturday, the first of September. School had just begun, and excitement in Polk High was at an all-time high—but not for our bass fishing team, of course, but for our football team. The Polk High Panthers were ranked #1 in the state and were projected to win the coveted Texas state football championship.

Every year Polk High had an amazing football team, but this year was different. Senior Quarterback Desmond Ward was at the helm. Desmond was all-state as a junior, stood 6'5", and had already accepted a college scholarship to play football at Texas A&M.

He was a legend at Polk, and he knew it. He loved it and ate up every ounce of attention he got from everyone. I would always joke with Eddie that I didn't know how Des could fit through the school's front doors with such a big head. Treated like a hero everywhere he went, he was cocky and arrogant.

I didn't care that he could throw a football 65 yards on one knee. I wasn't impressed with the record-setting 40 touchdown passes he had as a junior. I wasn't impressed with Desmond Ward—at least not anymore.

Desmond and I had been best friends all through elementary school. We were basically inseparable. Every birthday party or sleepover, we'd always be together. We spent most of our Saturdays together playing outside until the eighth grade. That's when Desmond hit his growth spurt and started to dominate on the gridiron. I didn't go out for football that year. We gradually stopped hanging out and talking. I guess we didn't have as much in common anymore. I wasn't prepared for the way the stardom affected Desmond. He acted like he was better than I was. The last time we hung out was awkward, and it was obvious that too many things had changed for our relationship to work anymore.

It was a sad time for me. I didn't know how to handle the feelings of losing my best friend.

Then isolation turned to teasing. Whenever I saw him and his jock buddies, he would make jokes and seem to sneer at me. He wasn't nice. He wasn't the same kid I had grown up with.

I wanted nothing more to do with Des. I avoided him in the hallways, classes, and lunchroom. Other people could worship him; I just avoided him.

Little did I know that my world was about to be turned upside down by the future college star.

-3-

The fall of my senior year was going to be the highlight of my high school experience. I was finally getting noticed and respected around the state's fishing circuits. Eddie and I spent most of the summer hitting some of the smaller lakes around Polk. We fished every day. Not a day went by that summer when we weren't on the water together.

We weren't the only ones preparing and planning for something magical. The football team was putting in some serious work as well. Every time I passed our school's football field, the players were working out. Guys were running, lifting weights, and throwing the football around to get ready for the upcoming season.

Our school was huge. My graduating class had over 1,000 kids, so it was easy to hide from Des and the rest of the football players. Eddie and I had a group of friends who went to all the games.

Even though many of the players were meatheads and thought of themselves as having some kind of celebrity status, it was kind of strange that the rest of us were still drawn to the Friday night lights.

We loved to watch and cheer on the Panthers. Football is part of our culture, so even though I didn't play, I still loved to watch and analyze the game. Of course, enjoying the games was nothing like my love for bass fishing!

The first week of school went by fast, and Friday finally arrived. I was sitting in my seventh-hour chemistry class when the PA speaker crackled, signaling our principal, Mr. Bakken. He liked to make an announcement giving the students the information about the football game. He focused on details like how to get to the game, where to park, and the exact time of kickoff.

His Friday announcement had become a Polk High tradition that every student looked forward to because it meant the teachers would have to stop their lessons. Afterward, all the football players would stand up and bang their chest or do something manly as other students cheered and encouraged them.

"Congratulations on completing your first week of school! I just wanted to take a moment to wish our football team good luck and give some details about tonight's game versus the Fayetteville Lions. Game time is 7:00 sharp, and fans can park and tailgate in the west parking lot. Thank you and rip 'em up, Panthers," he shouted as the entire room burst out in cheers.

Every Friday since I had been a freshman, it was the same voice and the same battle cry at the end. Mr. Bakken always talked about the football team, whether on the loudspeaker or in conversation. All other sports played second fiddle to football. It was just something we had all gotten used to.

This football game was going to be a big deal, especially since it was the first game of the year against crosstown rival Fayetteville.

Eddie and I had a big event this weekend too—the first high school bass fishing tournament at the Fayetteville County Reservoir. It was the Texas High School Bass Kickoff Classic, with over 50 Texas high schools participating. Last year, Eddie and I placed fourteenth out of 150 teams.

I was certain Mr. Bakken and the rest of the school didn't know or didn't care.

-4-

The atmosphere at the football game was electric. The sportscaster announced that attendance was around 20,000 people. *Can you believe that many people would watch a bunch of high school kids run and tackle each other?*

This game was super exciting, which added even more drama to the game. Football is a complicated sport, but I loved the strategy behind calling the offensive plays. It was like a chess match. When I was bored, I had a hobby of drawing and doodling a new passing play I thought would work. It was fun to sketch out various formations and draw plays and decide where to put the tight ends and wideouts. I also sometimes liked to sketch a bass ripping at my lure.

The actual game started at 7:00 p.m., but most people arrived a couple of hours earlier. The smell of barbecued pork and chicken surrounded the tailgating tents, trucks, and RVs. Fans played corn hole and ring toss. Everyone has fun.

We always tailgated with the same group of people. Eddie's dad owned an RV company and brought the biggest and best motor home on his lot. They had a huge spread of food, and hundreds of people met there before the game.

Mr. Bakken was always there too. Eddie's dad and Mr. Bakken were old high school football buddies and had graduated from Polk High. They were teammates on one of Polk High's best football teams. The team lost a heartbreaker 21-20 in the state championship but won second place. It seems like that was all they ever talked about.

They would always say things like, "Remember that play…" or "That one time when Coach did this or that…." Their stories were entertaining at first, but I had heard the same stories many times over the past two years. However, there was a lot of positive energy, and the food was fabulous.

The first football game of the season wasn't going to disappoint any fans. It was a thriller going back and forth. Late in the fourth quarter, Desmond dropped back to pass on a fourth and long and found our wide receiver Jimmy Wright on a fly pattern down the sideline. The touchdown pass put the Panthers up 38-32 and proved to be the game winner.

Desmond was nearly perfect in the game, completing 25 of 28 passes including five touchdowns. He was a big-armed quarterback who wasn't afraid to stand in the pocket and deliver a rocket to one of his receivers downfield.

Fireworks erupted in the sky, spraying a multitude of colors over the stadium. The Polk football team had a long list of sports boosters, so money was never an issue when it came to the football team. They got the best of everything. The football stadium resembled a college field with the latest technology, including video monitors and artificial turf.

When the game ended, the action continued. Adults and kids went out to celebrate afterward with most of them heading down to Pizza World. The restaurant served more pizza and breadsticks on a Friday night than they did all week. It was the place everyone went. Polk High Panther jerseys hung on the wall from the past thirty years of football glory.

Desmond had his own shrine. Right above the cash register, both his home and away jersey were displayed with an autographed 8 x 10 picture.

There was no way Eddie and I were going to Pizza World tonight. We had a big day in the morning. It was the start of our bid to win the state championship.

Even though we didn't sign any autographs or get to eat for free at Pizza World, it was pretty important to us. Our boat had to be on the water by 7:00 am.

The bass fishing tournament was going to be a busy time, and Eddie and I were going to land some giants. I planned on putting on a show much like Desmond Ward had done the night before, only I would be flinging lures and spinners instead of footballs.

-5-

The next morning I picked up Eddie at his house, and we headed towards the reservoir, about a 45-minute drive. Talking with him was easy. Our conversation revolved around last night's football game and our plans for bass fishing that morning.

"Desmond sure is something," Eddie said.

I sighed and rolled my eyes at the same time. "Of course he is—one of the best ever to play at Polk."

Every time Desmond Ward was mentioned, I felt an ache in the pit of my stomach. Eddie knew I didn't particularly like Desmond, but I never went into much detail as to why I couldn't stand him. Most of the time Desmond said or did something to make himself look like an egotistical maniac—at least that's what I told myself. I was sure I wasn't the only kid walking around Polk High who didn't like the great Desmond Ward.

"I hear he's a lock for the NFL," Eddie offered.

"We'll see. He's his own worst enemy. Who told you he could make the National Football League? Desmond tell you that?" I asked, a little irritated at the thought.

"No, I was reading some of the different recruiting websites. He's the highest-ranked quarterback in Texas history. The only high school quarterback recruits ranked higher were Drew Brees and Patrick Mahomes. Both of those guys will be in the NFL Hall of Fame."

"Good for him," I said, showing my frustration.

"Why do you hate him so much?"

"I don't hate him. I just don't like him much." I didn't want to talk about Desmond and ruin our day.

"I saw those pictures in your room of you guys laughing and hanging out when you were younger. What happened?"

"He got cool. He became the legendary Desmond Ward, and I stunk at football," I said quietly.

That small amount of information was enough for Eddie, and he quickly changed the subject to Vicky Vermont, the captain of the cheerleading squad.

"I just love her," he said with a big smile.

"Good luck! You have a better chance of catching the game-winning touchdown pass from Des than you do of having Vicky as a girlfriend."

"Ha…I don't even play football; that's impossible!"

"Exactly," I quipped back, and we both burst out laughing.

When we arrived at the fishing competition, the parking lot was already packed with boats and trailers. We headed down to the picturesque lake and admired the reflections on the water as the morning sun painted the waves a pale yellow.

Eddie got out and prepped the boat, getting it ready to launch from a nearby dock. I watched in the rearview mirror, and once I got the thumbs up, I slowly backed the trailer into the water.

Within minutes, the boat was safely in the water, and I was parking the truck. We had done this so many times before that we had it down to a science.

Eddie and the boat were waiting near the dock, and I promptly jumped in. We often fished this lake and knew about a great bass habitat near the west side.

The roar of the Evinrude engine put a smile on my face. I looked at Eddie; he was smiling too. I wasn't sure if he was excited about fishing or was still daydreaming about Vicky.

Either way, it didn't matter to me. I was in my happy place on my bass boat.

-6-

The fishing started out slow on Saturday. Mid-morning, we hooked into some nice bass but nothing big enough to put us on the leader board. The rules for the high school tournaments were all the same; the judges take the combined weight of each team's biggest five fish.

Saturday's contest had a required 3:15 check-in time for weighing. Anyone who weighed their fish in after that would be disqualified from that day's catch. We reported to the station at 3:00 with a combined weight of 30 pounds, which gave us a six-pound average.

The team that was in first place was from Carmine High School. The Bears of Carmine High had a great tradition when it came to high school bass fishing. They usually won league, districts, and regionals, and the school finished in the top three at state every year. This year seemed to be their year to win state because they were led by twins Jeff and Jack Jones, sons of a professional bass fishing Texas legend. They were only sophomores but were already unbelievable fishermen.

Their first day's catch included three nice-sized fish and two giants. Their five fish weighed 60 pounds, giving them a 12-pound average. Their biggest fish was just shy of 16 pounds.

The judges weigh and record every fish individually. Our biggest fish weighed in at 14 pounds. Our only hope to place higher in the tournament was to have a great catch on Sunday. We knew we would at least have to replace four of our five fish.

When the fishermen are out on the water, the fish they catch are kept in a live well that has an aerator pumping fresh air into the water. After the official weigh-in, a judge walks each team down to a spot on the shore to release their fish. The trauma from being caught usually causes the fish to take a few days break from biting any lures again.

Eddie and I have a certain way we like to release our bass. We do it slowly, taking a little extra time to see that each bass is okay before we let it go. We want to make sure it can survive being set free.

I wasn't worried; I knew we would find some fish on Sunday. I had no plans on starting our senior fishing season with anything less than a top ten finish.

We had six tournaments, which all counted towards the state championship. At the end of the season, the top ten teams have a huge weekend bass tournament on Lake Somerville right after Thanksgiving.

Eddie and I knew that every ounce counts with every fish because the cumulative points matter. We knew we had to be focused and ready to try some new approaches to get back on the top ten board.

As we were releasing the last fish, I heard a pair of footsteps coming up behind us. I turned and saw the Jones twins looking impatiently in our direction.

"You *ladies* about done?" Jeff mocked us.

"Excuse me?" I quickly shot back.

I was surprised that a sophomore thought he could talk to a senior like that. I knew who they were but had never met them in person.

"You heard me. You can stop babying those fish. We got things to do," Jack demanded.

Shocked, I turned, looking at Eddie who was trying not to make eye contact with the Jones twins.

When I turned back to say something to the obnoxious brothers, I felt a hard whack on the side of my head. The blow hit me so hard, it knocked off my sunglasses and hat.

Jeff had thrown one of their fish directly at me. I tried to shrug it off and not look weak, but my head hurt. I looked down and saw a gorgeous olive- and dark-green colored largemouth bass flailing on the ground. The fish was struggling to breathe with its gills moving in and out at a rapid pace.

I picked up the fish and quickly threw it into deeper water. *Game on...*

-7-

I took two large steps towards Jeff when the judge grabbed me.

"Not here, boys. Any altercation will disqualify all your points from this tournament," he warned.

I glared at Jeff. A large vein in my forehead throbbed as my face turned bright red. I was so mad I thought I was going to burst.

"Let's go, Rock. These bozos aren't worth it," Eddie declared, pulling me back towards the truck.

As we walked away, I could hear both boys making jokes and laughing as they released the rest of their fish. I was upset that upset that he had hit me with the fish, but what really pushed me over the top was the way he had treated the fish. He didn't respect his catch, and that total disregard really bothered me.

On the drive back to Polk, Eddie and I decided to use a different topwater lure and try an area of the lake that wasn't known to have an abundance of fish. We knew there were some hidden spots with submerged brush and trees that probably hadn't been fished much Saturday. We also agreed to be on the lake an hour earlier in the morning. The place we wanted to fish was a bit of a drive, and we both knew we didn't have a lot of time to waste.

I tried to pass off the fish incident, but I was still fuming inwardly. The Jones brothers lit a fire in me, and I made up my mind I wasn't going to let them embarrass me again.

The next morning, I was startled by the loud, annoying sound of my alarm clock. It seemed like I had just fallen asleep.

On the way to Eddie's house, I couldn't help but replay yesterday's fish-throwing incident. I knew I had to let go of my bad feelings toward the Jones brothers, or we would start the season off low on the leader board. This was a team sport, and I owed it to Eddie to focus on fishing.

"Good morning, Sunshine," I greeted as Eddie climbed into my truck.

"Morning," he mumbled.

Eddie usually was excited and happy to get up on Saturday mornings, but Sundays were always tough on him. He looked tired, and I could tell he needed an energy boost.

I reached down and turned the radio station to a classic rock station and cranked up the volume. Rock 'n' roll filled the truck, and the bass and treble were pumping. That noise started to wake up Eddie.

The parking lot was almost still empty when we first pulled in. Dawn was just breaking by the time we unloaded the boat and completed our safety checks.

As we motored across the lake, I turned back to the marina and could see the glow of truck head-lights. Vehicles were starting to fill up the parking lot.

Ten minutes later, we roared towards the south

side of the lake when we noticed another boat trailing closely behind us.

"Of course," I grumbled.

"Who is it?" asked Eddie.

Without even turning around, I knew.

"It's Jeff and Jack," I said.

- 8 -

I divided my attention between the GPS and the compass that sat on top of the console near the steering wheel. We had plotted some good spots earlier in the summer, and that was where we were starting.

After a couple of minutes, I heard Eddie say something. I turned.

"Huh?" I said.

"They're gone; they turned off a while back," Eddie yelled.

I was relieved but carried on like it was no big deal. The last thing I wanted was another altercation with the Jones brothers, but there was no way I was going to let Eddie know that.

Motoring at full throttle for another ten minutes,

we finally reached the spot we planned on fishing. The water was calm, and the sky was slightly overcast. Cloudy days are some of the best days for bass action. They give anglers a prime window to catch a big bass. We also knew the reservoir waters would be slightly muddy from a short rain in the middle of the night.

Eddie and I started with some darker purple and black spinnerbaits. We knew the fish liked the action of the spinnerbait, especially on dreary mornings.

The first couple casts of the morning are always my favorite. They remind me of Christmas morning when you walk downstairs and see the lit tree surrounded by presents.

On my third cast, I had a hard hit on my line. I quickly reeled, nothing. I cast it back towards the spot where something had hit. BAM!

This time, the fish hit the lure harder, and I knew I had hooked a nice-sized bass. I could feel the weight of the fish and knew it was bigger than any fish I had caught the day before. I battled the fish for a couple of minutes. It made one more strong run before I was able to reel it in.

Eddie grabbed it and weighed it on our small portable electric scale. Although not official, it gave us a good indicator of the weight of each fish.

The fish weighed 14.3 pounds and was our prize catch of the weekend so far. Even if I didn't catch another fish, I was thankful to get such a good one. Eddie reeled in a nice largemouth thirty minutes later that hit the scales at just under 12 pounds. I knew we would move up the leader board with these two fish but felt we would need at least one more fish over 11 pounds to make the top ten cut. We fished the first spot for another hour before reeling in our lines.

"We got one more shot to make this happen," Eddie reminded me.

"I know. I think we should try North Island."

"That's quite a ways from here, Rock. Do you think we have the time to go that far to fish?"

"I don't think we can afford not to. It's the only other spot I can think of that could have a big one.

Let's do it!" I shouted, firing up the motor. It took us another hour until we arrived across the reservoir at North Island.

I looked at my watch, and we only had about thirty minutes to fish before we had to leave. The weigh-in time is specific, and they don't allow any late entries for any reason.

I had just started switching out my topwater lures, when Eddie hooked into a big fish. The force of the fish caused his rod to bend in a way that made me think it was a snag at first. North Island was known for having lots of sunken trees and debris, common places to get snags. He reeled and rocked the rod and suddenly felt a tug back. It was a fish—a big one!

Eddie is cool under pressure, but I could see the excitement and anticipation in his face. Whatever it was, it was much bigger than anything we had hooked the entire weekend.

As the fish got closer to the boat, I could make out a solid outline.

I was shocked at its size.

"Grab the net!" Eddie yelled.

I stumbled back to the stern of the boat to retrieve it. I carefully slipped the big, green net into the water and around the fish.

It took all my strength to pull the fish out of the water. My back heaved as I turned and flipped the fish onto the boat.

Eddie had just caught a monster!

-9-

Unfortunately, it was a monster catfish…

The brute's whiskers extended outside its big, square tank-like head. I would guess the fish was pushing 25-30 pounds. It was the biggest fish we had ever caught on our bass boat. Of course the excitement wore off when we saw it wasn't a bass.

"Still a cool fish to catch," I consoled Eddie.

"Yeah, that was an awesome fight. I thought it was a bass, though. It won't really help us score today."

The only fish that counted for the weigh-in were each team's top five bass.

"That was a great fight, no matter. Can't get too upset about landing a fish like that." Eddie nodded in agreement.

I walked over to the glove box of the boat and grabbed some needle-nose pliers. I picked up the catfish and used the pliers to remove the hook.

After I released the fish over the starboard side of the boat, we watched as the catfish swam away.

We spent the next twenty minutes intensely casting with a couple of hits but didn't land anything. We knew we had a decent number but weren't sure it was enough to get us into the top ten.

We pulled the boat up to the dock with five minutes to spare as a judge walked over to weigh our fish.

After the fish were weighed and recorded, Eddie and I went to release them. I heard a loud cheer coming from the crowd as the announcer congratulated the first place team of Jeff and Jack Jones.

The Bears win again…

We ended up getting ninth place, which was a great spot to be in, considering our struggles from the first day of fishing.

We were called on stage for a picture and to receive our medals. The Jones brothers didn't look in our direction, but I knew they would be a problem the entire year. But I didn't work this hard during my last year in high school to let two sophomores steal my glory.

I had to admit, those boys knew how to fish, but so did we. I knew as long as Eddie and I stuck together, we were going to beat the Jones brothers. Even though we didn't win today, we both knew we were on the right track.

We were sure we had what it took to win the whole thing.

-10-

Over the next couple of weeks, time flew by. The football team continued to win, and Eddie and I did well in the last couple of bass tournaments. We finished fourth in the Austin Bass Classic and won a much smaller competition on Lake Bastrop.

We were in the top five in the state for points with three tournaments remaining. As long as we stayed in the top ten, we would get the invite for the Texas Bass Master Championship on Lake Somerville—our goal since we had started fishing together.

We wanted a chance to fish Lake Somerville and bring home Polk High School's first bass fishing state championship. Coming close wasn't going to cut it this year. This was my last chance to leave my mark on high school and accomplish what no one else at our school had ever done.

The football team was halfway to their state championship with two blowout victories. In the last game, Des had thrown six touchdowns and became the all-time leader in passing touchdowns at Polk. This year alone, he had thrown 13 touchdowns without an interception.

The next couple of games weren't even close. The Panthers were looking like they had a team that could win the state championship. Polk High School had been the state runner-up several times, taking second place four times. They had taken second place on two occasions when Eddie's dad and Mr. Bakken had played together.

The whole town felt that this was finally the year they were going to bring home the big one. Polk High could be Texas' next football state champions.

The following weekend fishing tournament was going to be important and exciting. Gibbons Creek Reservoir was hosting the bass tournament, and schools from across the state were going to compete. The tournament's grand prize was what drew the most attention. The winner of the G.C.R. Bass Challenge received two gigantic trophies that stood over six feet tall.

When I was younger, I dreamed about hoisting up that trophy. The winning team would have instant credibility throughout the state and the entire south.

The G.C.R. Bass Challenge was one of the biggest high school bass fishing tournaments in the United States. Some really big largemouth bass called the reservoir home. The fishing was excellent, but the winning team was going to have to work for it.

More than 200 two-person teams had entered the competition. The challenge of so many boats plying the waters just upped the pressure of the G.C.R. The abundance of competition made it harder to hook into a large bass and limited the number of good places to fish. Often, anglers were fishing right next to other boats.

Last year the winning team had a five fish combined score of 58 pounds. In other tournaments, Eddie and I hit 60-65 pounds, but that probably wasn't going to happen at the G.C.R.

Even with all the amazing incentives for winning, I wanted to win for two bigger reasons. I looked at the trophy and the notoriety as just an added bonus. The first was that the winning team automatically received an invitation to compete at the state championships at Lake Somerville. We had been doing well in points but didn't have a guarantee to make it to the state championship.

It didn't matter how the winners of the G.C.R. fished the rest of the season; they received a golden ticket to the state championship. I wanted that more than anything. But that wasn't my only motivation.

I also wanted to get revenge on the Jones brothers. I had been following them online, and they were doing well, finishing in the top three at almost every fishing tournament. I hadn't seen them since our last run-in when they threw the fish at me, but

I knew they would be there. Nothing was more important to them than winning at Gibbons Creek. They would love to brag and strut around with those huge trophies.

They valued the glitz and the glamour even more than the fishing, so I looked forward to when they watched Eddie and I walk up on stage and pose for pictures with the giant trophies. Revenge was even more of an incentive than winning the golden ticket, but I planned on enjoying every second of it when it happened.

I had envisioned this victory for months. All I had to do was convince Eddie and stick to our fishing skills. I didn't realize that one of those would be much harder than I ever imagined.

-11-

This Friday at school was going much like the previous ones, with a lot of talk and excitement revolving around the football game. Every once in a while, a teacher would ask me about the fishing tournament. Eddie and I started getting some attention in our local paper, but most of the school didn't know or didn't care.

Eddie and I chatted over lunch when my cellphone buzzed. I glanced down and noticed a weather report calling for high winds and possible storms for Saturday and Sunday.

"What's up?" Eddie asked as I scanned the emergency weather report.

"Hmm. Looks like this weekend is going to be

more challenging than we thought. We have some nasty weather coming in, possible storms and high winds."

I could fish anytime, anywhere, and in almost any weather conditions, but no way would we be out on the water if lightning began. High winds, on the other hand, made fishing tough but not impossible.

Unfortunately, I never had much luck fishing in windy conditions. It seemed to me that the fish didn't bite as well. It was also much harder to cast and feel a good bite.

Managing the boat was also a major issue in high winds. It usually didn't anchor well or stay in one spot. Eddie and I liked to tuck in and fish near little inlets that had downed timber. The big largemouths loved hanging out in the submerged trees that provided good coverage for them from predators.

"Do you want to just cancel?" Eddie asked, his eyebrows raised.

I turned and gave him a long, drawn-out stare. He knew what it meant.

There was no way I wasn't going to compete at the G.C.R., especially with the Jones boys going. I didn't care if a hurricane, tornado, or tropical storm was coming—we were fishing this tournament!

That night in bed I could see the shaking silhouette of our family's huge oak tree outside my window whipping in the wind. The branches creaked and moaned as the wind bellowed through its branches.

I had trouble sleeping. I knew the next morning would come quickly, but my mind was racing. *What was I going to say when I saw the Jones brothers?* I couldn't let them disrespect me again. *And how would we launch the boat if the wind was blowing hard at the dock?*

The last image I remember seeing before falling asleep was the Jones brothers getting blown off their boats and into the cold water.

When the alarm on my phone blared, I crawled out of bed. It took me a couple of minutes to get my bearings and clear the sleep from my eyes. I had a slight headache from a lack of sleep. I scrambled to my feet, got dressed, and grabbed a granola bar as I headed out the front door.

As soon as I opened up the front door, I knew there were going to be problems. The wind whipped my face and slammed the screen door several times before I could corral it.

I checked my phone to make sure the tournament hadn't been canceled and loaded up my truck. I drove across town and picked up Eddie. I could feel the truck and trailer swaying back and forth with each wind gust. The drive to the G.C.R. in the dark gave us time to go over our fishing plans for the weekend. I could tell Eddie was nervous.

"Rock, maybe we should just go back home. I mean it's really windy out," he pointed out.

"Go home? Are you crazy? This is our chance to stuff it down the Jones brothers' throat!"

He sat quietly at first. "Is that the reason why you're so insistent on us fishing this weekend? Are you fishing because you want to get revenge on the Jones brothers?"

"No…I just want to…" cutting myself off as I checked my true motive.

That's when I knew that Eddie was right, and I was wrong. My primary motivation was to get back at the Jones brothers, and my objective was making me bitter. Eddie deserved better than that.

"You're right, Eddie. I'm sorry, man. The idea of revenge is the wrong reason to do anything. If it's too dangerous when we get there, we'll turn around and go back home."

When we pulled into the G.C.R. Marina, I knew something strange was going on. Not many boats or trailers were in the parking lot. Only about 25 percent of the usual teams had arrived.

"This is odd," I whispered.

One of the judges walked up to our window as we neared the dock. "Name and high school?"

"Is the tournament canceled?" I asked.

"Not yet, but it looks like a lot of teams have dropped out already," the judge explained. "In the tournament guidelines, it states the only reason we cancel is for hazardous weather. The bylaws state that lightning is the only weather-related condition to warrant cancellation. Nothing in the bylaws mentions high winds. So per the rules, we plan on sticking it out."

"Maybe we should just go home then, Rock."

"Sir, do you know if the Jones brothers have checked in?" I asked.

The judge turned and scanned his list.

"Nope, they were one of the teams that called and scratched this morning. It looks like we only have about twenty teams participating," he said as he scanned his clipboard.

"Just another reason for us to go home…" murmured Eddie.

"We're in!" I said confidently to the judge.

"Okay, boys, go ahead and unload the boat. Good luck and stay safe," he added.

"Rock, tell me why are we staying."

I sat still for a minute, listening to the wind whistling through the front of the truck.

"Eddie, this could be a blessing in disguise. Did you hear what the judge said? There are only about 20 teams competing—that's 10 percent of the original 200 teams. Do you know what that means? We have a way better chance of winning and punching our ticket to Lake Somerville!"

"I don't think I'm comfortable with this, Rock. I think we just need to go home."

"Sorry, Eddie. We're staying and winning this tournament," I declared and added, "I think Vicky is going to be really impressed when you show her your giant trophy!"

He sat and thought for a minute.

"You really think she would?" he asked.

Hook, line, and sinker...

-12-

Unloading the trailer that day was a crazy experience in itself. I had never fished in such high winds, plus the rain started as soon as the trailer hit the water. But there weren't any thunderstorms or lightning.

As I walked down the dock, I could see a couple of boats already on the water. *If they could do it, then why couldn't Eddie and I?*

"Are you sure about this?" Eddie asked for the hundredth time, checking to see if I had changed my mind.

"Undo the cargo straps and get the boat in the water. We can do this," I assured him.

The wind whipped Eddie and swayed the trailer as I backed it into the water. The splatter of the rain made a rhythmic sound, resembling an 80s rock band.

It took a little longer than usual, but Eddie finally launched the boat, and I parked the truck. Thankfully, the wind was at our back as we roared away from the dock. I knew that we would have to come in with the bow of the boat into the wind when we returned.

We had never fished this lake before, so we were going on pure instinct. We had done our research and plotted out some good possible points on our map. We knew that there were shallow places near the back of the lake, but I wasn't sure if we could get to the mapped-out spots with the high winds.

It was so windy that we decided to go to the second spot Eddie had found on the map. We liked how the water thinned out before a big drop-off and figured that was as good of a place as any to start fishing.

We attempted to anchor but got pushed back out into open water. We were going to have to use two anchors to get the boat to stand still. I told Eddie to pull his line. I moved the boat and anchored so the wind was at our back, allowing us to cast towards a big fallen oak tree that stretched about 30 feet in the water.

The flag on the stern of our boat was flailing in the wind. I had thought it was windy when we started out, but now the wind had picked up even more. Without warning, the flag ripped and went flying across the lake. I was fiddling with the anchor when I heard Eddie yell out. "I got one, Rock. It's a decent one too!"

I scrambled over with the net as he battled the fish closer to the boat. I scooped the largemouth up in the net just as his crankbait came loose, slipping out of the fish's mouth.

"Wow! That was close!" Eddie sighed in relief.

"Great job, man! This is a nice fish," I told him. We weighed the fish in at 10.6 pounds. As the wind picked up, so did the rain. It suddenly came down sideways, making it difficult to see any landmarks.

Eddie put the fish in the live well.

"Eddie, I think maybe we should head back. Something isn't right," I said as I glanced up at the sky.

"Fine by me, man. I'm ready to go."

As soon as those words left his mouth, both of our cell phones starting making an extremely loud, unique sound. It was another weather warning, but this time it was an emergency warning.

"A tornado?" Eddie asked.

I nodded. "Looks like it's heading right towards us." I quickly turned the key, and thankfully, the engine roared to life. I pushed and pushed the accelerator but had trouble making headway as we tried to steer towards the dock. The headwind was even stronger, and it felt like we were moving in slow motion.

Because of the wind blowing behind us, it had only taken about 20 minutes to get out to our fishing spot. Going against the wind would make it at least double that to return. Eddie was watching the storm on his phone as it roared towards the lake.

Our parents were texting both of us as well, and we reassured them we were aware of the storm and taking cover. We didn't mention that we were still on the water. We had only fished for about ten minutes before the storm overtook us. As I drove the boat back, with the wind and rain pounding on my face, I had to face a stark reality—Eddie had been right; going out in this weather was a bad idea. I had let my thoughts of revenge against the Jones brothers push us to a place we shouldn't have ever been.

A tornado was bearing down on us, even though it wasn't in the original forecast. A sharp pain started in the pit of my stomach. I knew it was a reminder, a signal that I knew better.

I knew the high winds were dangerous, and we should have stayed home. I knew we were in big trouble, and it was all my fault.

-13-

I was an experienced captain, but I had never piloted a boat in such a strong headwind. The cold, hard rain felt like tiny needles stinging my face.

I was thankful for our GPS. Without it, we would have been in even more danger. I was dependent on the fact that the coordinates were correct as it guided us back to the dock. Otherwise, I would have had no idea of where to go in the storm.

Our situation was tense; I could tell Eddie was not happy about going out. But I didn't have time to apologize or worry; I had to get us back to land safely.

It seemed like it took forever, but eventually, I could make out the glowing lights of the dock. When we pulled in, I jumped out and ran for the truck.

Eddie prepared the boat as I slowly backed down the loading ramp. The wind was pushing the truck, and I struggled to straighten the trailer. I did the best that I could, but Eddie had to work hard to keep the boat from smashing into the side of the dock. He was masterful on the boat's throttle, keeping it in place.

He was skilled, and I was lucky to have him as my partner. He had to go from neutral and then hammer the accelerator to reposition the boat. A lesser boat-man would have smashed the boat into the dock.

Somehow I got the trailer close enough, and he zipped the boat onto the trailer. I hopped out and started strapping it down. We crawled back into the truck, drenched, and breathing heavy. We had survived, but I knew we should have never taken the risk.

As I slowly drove up the ramp, only three cars were in the parking lot. My foot pressed firmly on the gas pedal as the truck hit the pavement clear of the boat ramp. Mentally I was already heading home.

"Stop!" Eddie's cold hand grasped my arm.

"What? We need to get out of here!" I shouted.

"The fish, the bass—it's still in the live well. We can't leave it in there; it'll die," Eddie shouted.

I nodded. He was right. It was our obligation to the fish to release it. Eddie got out and climbed up into the trailer and got in the boat.

I was sitting looking in the rearview mirror, watching Eddie to make sure he was safe. Suddenly the judge who had checked us in earlier that morning knocked on my window.

"Well, that was a wild one," I said.

"Glad you boys are okay. You're the last boat to come in," he said. "What's your buddy doing? Shouldn't he be in the truck with you?"

"Yeah, we had caught a nice one, and he's going to toss it back in before we go," I said.

"Wait, you guys caught a bass?" the judge asked.

"Yeah, we caught one. Why?" I couldn't figure out why he wanted to know.

"Is it over 9 pounds?" the judge asked.

As soon as I said, "It was 10-something…" the judge took off running and shouting at Eddie.

-14-

"Stop! Stop! Don't release that fish yet!" yelled the judge through the pounding rain.

The rain and wind made it hard to hear, and Eddie was just about to launch the bass back into the water when he caught movement behind him.

"Let me weigh that fish!" the judge shouted out to Eddie.

"Why?"

"Trust me. Just follow me to my truck," the judge ordered.

Eddie motioned for me to follow, so I pulled up and parked the truck.

"Sir, what's this all about?" I asked.

"Boys, according to the Texas state rules, once

a tournament starts, any fish that are caught and weighed in before it is canceled have to be counted, and a winner awarded. Up to now, the biggest fish was a nine pounder," he said, putting our bass on the scale.

I stood still in shock. The rain was letting up slightly, but it was still a chaotic atmosphere.

"Do you know what that means, Rock?" Eddie yelled over to me.

It still hadn't registered. I was trying to understand all the events from the day and hadn't caught on to what the judge meant.

"Rock, that means we have punched our ticket to the state championship!" cried Eddie.

"What?" I couldn't believe it.

The judge called us over to the wooden pavilion that housed all the tournament information. Once there, he handed us two gigantic trophies and a small, laminated slip of paper.

"Congrats, boys, you're going to be at the state championship in three weeks at Lake Somerville. According to the rules, you are the official winners of the G.C.R. Bass Championship. Keep this piece of paper, and you'll both get letters in the mail outlining the information for the state championship. I know the weather was horrible, but you guys are going back to Polk with some hardware," said the judge.

We thanked him, and trophies in hand, we hurried back to the truck.

"Hey, Rock, give me your trophy, and I'll put them both in the back of the truck."

I handed it to him and climbed in, quickly starting the truck. I watched as Eddie carried both trophies. He looked funny since the trophies were taller than he was, but then Eddie slipped on the wet pavement and lost his footing. Instead of using his arms to stop his fall, he tightly gripped the trophies to prevent them from being broken. He landed hard.

I jumped out of the vehicle and ran around the truck. When I reached him, he was moaning in pain, but miraculously, the trophies were intact.

"Eddie, are you okay?" I shouted over the slashing rain.

At first, he just rolled around in pain. Then he looked up at me. "I hurt my arms," he explained.

"Why didn't you just drop the trophies?"

"Are you kidding me? I plan on showing this to Vicky on Monday. No way was I dropping mine."

When he had landed, he stuck both of his arms straight up so the trophies wouldn't break. But by doing so, he landed hard on his elbow and lower arm.

I helped him up and loaded the trophies as he crawled into the passenger seat. I got in and smiled at him. "Well, what a day! Huh, partner? I can't wait to show my parents this trophy and tell them the good news."

About ten minutes into our return ride home as I focused intently on driving, Eddie spoke up. "Can we make a stop before going home?"

"Do you want me to swing by Vicky's house?" I asked, chuckling.

"No…I think we should stop at the hospital emergency room." He gritted his teeth in obvious pain.

-15-

I wheeled the truck into Huntsville Memorial Hospital and called Eddie's mom. The farther we had gone, the clearer it became that something was terribly wrong with Eddie. I ran around the other side of the truck, opened his door, and helped him out.

As soon as we entered the hospital, a nurse came to put Eddie in a wheelchair. Within minutes, she pushed him through two huge metal doors into the emergency room.

After calling Eddie's parents, all I could do was sit and wait in my soaking-wet clothes. As I waited, my guilt grew.

About a half hour later, his parents arrived, and I told them what had happened. They could tell I was still shaken and had a huge sense of guilt for dragging Eddie to the fishing tournament.

"Rock, accidents like this happen," Eddie's dad reassured me. "He'll be fine. You better head home. We have it from here, son. We'll call you when we know something."

Reluctantly I got up and went out to my truck. I had to park it at the back of the parking lot because the bass boat was still attached. The wind had let up now, and as I turned on the radio, the host mentioned a tornado touching down about 15 miles east of where we had been fishing.

I drove home, feeling bad about Eddie's accident. In my rearview mirror, I noticed the giant trophies still sitting in the back. I swung by Eddie's house and took his trophy inside his garage, setting it by the door that led into the house. I thought it might make him smile a little when he got home. I drove home, wet and guilt-ridden.

After lunch, I sat down on my bed and started scrolling through my cell phone. Suddenly a text message came through, and there was a picture of Eddie in the emergency room with both of his arms in hard casts. His message read, "Both arms are broken. I'm out of commission for six to eight weeks."

I sent him a smiley emoji and told him I was sorry and was praying for him.

My eyes started to well up, and a lone tear ran down my right cheek. I felt bad for Eddie, but his announcement meant that we were officially out of the state championship. It was only three weeks away, and my partner had two broken arms. There was no way he would be able to help me when it came to fishing.

Other kids were on the fishing team at Polk—one was a promising sophomore I had fished with who was pretty good. But without Eddie, I didn't want to compete anymore. Plus, every other member of the fishing team already had a partner. If I took one of them, someone else would be without a partner.

Nope, that was it. My dream of winning a high school state championship had ended when Eddie fell in the wet parking lot. The next day I called my coach and explained it to him. He was sad for Eddie and me. He offered a couple of ideas and mentioned talking to the team to see if he could move someone to fish with me.

I told him thanks, but I wasn't interested. My desire to compete was gone. The Jones brothers could have their way; I was done wasting my time trying to beat them. I told my coach to scratch us out of the last three tournaments.

I knew that Eddie got hurt because I was reckless. Not the senior year I had waited for—not at all…

-16-

The following week was going to be tough. I really didn't feel like going to school and listening to how awesome the football team was. On Monday, a couple of people at school told me they felt bad over what had happened.

I thanked them but didn't have much energy to respond further. I felt like a duck out of water anyway. Eddie was going to stay home for a while, leaving me without my best friend. I had other friends, but they didn't know me like Eddie. They didn't know the feeling of watching the sun rise on a bass boat or the rush I got when I hooked into a giant largemouth bass. Eddie got it; he loved it too.

During lunch on Friday, I sat at a table with a

couple of my buddies from math class. The football players were extra excited, and the school was a buzz. Tonight we played the Bellville Brahmas—our biggest rival. Both teams were undefeated, and the schools were only 15 minutes apart.

Most of the players knew each other, and it made the game even higher stakes. This was the first game of the playoffs for Polk. They would have to win the next three games to make it to the state championship at AT&T Stadium in Dallas.

Everyone at school was decked out in red and black. Even the faculty was wearing Polk football gear.

It seemed like football was all anyone cared about. Our bass fishing team had a tournament the next day, but it was too hard for me to go. I told Coach that I just couldn't. While he wasn't happy, he said he understood.

Deep down, I always looked forward to the football games, and tonight's game was sure to be a good one. I was also excited because I was meeting Eddie at the tailgate party. He had texted me and wanted to get together. I missed hanging out with him since I hadn't seen him after he broke his arms.

He did tell me he sent Vicky a picture of his trophy, and she was pretty impressed. I don't know if it helped, but he said it took away some of the pain.

I got to the tailgate party a little early and was happy to see Eddie was already there. He looked funny with both arms in casts all the way from his wrist to his elbows. The one on his right arm was red and the one on his left arm was black, honoring the Polk High Panthers.

We exchanged small talk at first, but I could tell he had something on his mind. I knew he wanted to tell me something.

"It wasn't your fault, Rock. I want you to know that. I really wish you would keep fishing on the team," he pleaded.

"Thanks, Eddie, but it just wouldn't be the same without you. There's no one I trust who can fish like you. You're done, and so am I."

"You could still go to State. Don't throw that away."

"I wouldn't have a chance without you. I'm not about to go and be the joke of Lake Somerville. I'm okay with it. Let the Jones brothers enjoy it."

"You still have three weeks until the tournament, Rock. I hope you change your mind."

"I doubt it." I shook my head at the thought.

Just then, his dad brought out a fresh batch of spicy Parmesan chicken wings. We laughed as his mom came over to help him eat. "You know, Rock, whatever works to keep a guy from starving…"

We started talking about the football game. I was anxious about the game and knew that Polk would have to play well to beat Bellville.

"They need to throw to the outside receivers 'cause that's where Bellville is weak," I told Eddie. "They're starting two sophomores at the cornerback position, and we're faster on the outside."

"Dude, you're a football genius. You always know what to do and where to do it against the other team. Maybe you'll be a coach someday." Eddie smiled.

"Thanks, but the only thing I'll probably ever coach is how to cast a spinner or topwater bait," I said and sighed.

That night was an epic night of Texas football. The stadium was packed and loud. Music boomed, and there wasn't an open seat anywhere in the stadium. The game went back and forth and was tied 27-27 late in the fourth quarter.

Bellville had the ball on our 20-yard line. On fourth and eight, they sent out their field goal kicker who boomed the football through the uprights, giving Bellville a three-point lead. After the kickoff return, Polk had the ball on the 34-yard line, still having 66 yards to go to win the game. Des dropped back to pass, but the ball was knocked down. On second down, Polk ran a running back screen that netted about ten yards, and they called their second time out.

"Watch this," I said to Eddie. "They'll double move on the outside; the cornerback has been playing shallow all game."

The Panthers jogged out after the timeout, and sure enough, Polk's outside receiver ran an out pattern, then turned it up field.

"Yes!" we both cried out together.

Des took a five-step drop and delivered a perfect pass that hit the receiver in stride as he jogged into the end zone.

Game over! Polk won 33-30!

- 17 -

Saturday morning was weird. Even though I wasn't fishing, I still woke up at 5:30 a.m., the time I usually would be hooking up the trailer and getting ready to pick up Eddie.

Not today, not again.

I moped around the house all morning and checked the weigh-in results of the tournament on the Internet. They were catching some nice fish, and the weather was perfect. Eddie and I would have loved it.

Being home on a Saturday during the fall was foreign to me since I was so used to fishing every weekend. I quickly realized I had to find something else to pass the time.

I grabbed the remote and turned it to college football. I was a diehard Texas Longhorn fan, so the game entertained me for the next four hours.

After lazing around for most of the day, my parents took us down to our family's favorite restaurant, The Popping Pig—the home of the world's best barbecue. I always got the same thing—Sassy Baby Back Ribs with some waffle fries. Even though the food was fantastic, it did little to improve my mood.

About halfway through dinner, a large number of football players came in to eat. I didn't know all of them, but one stood out and was easy to identify.

A tall guy strolled around the restaurant smiling, shaking hands, and posing for pictures. It was the quarterback, the superstar of the Polk High Panthers.

"Honey, there's your old friend Desi," my mom said. I rolled my eyes, I was sure no one had called him Desi since eighth grade.

"Mom…shhhhhh. Don't draw attention to us," I warned her.

"Okay, honey, but I thought it would be nice to

say hi and congratulations to him. Desi was always such a nice boy," she said.

"Yeah, he sure used to be," I mumbled to myself. My mom was still stuck in eighth grade mode, unaware of the changes and the evolution of Desmond Ward.

"I wouldn't mind a quick autograph, if he has a second," my dad said as he looked for a piece of paper.

"What? Please, no!" I said, disgusted.

Desmond must have seen my parents smiling and staring at him, so he made his way over to our table.

"Desi," my mom said.

"Hello. Mrs. Conrad, it's so nice to see you."

"Des, if you have a second, is there any way you could sign my menu?" asked my dad. "I'd love an autograph of a future NFL quarterback."

Earlier in the day, I had told myself things couldn't get worse. I must have lied. Not only was I embarrassed, I was angry. My rage boiled as I sat there watching Des sign my dad's menu.

Before he walked away, he turned towards me. "Hey, Rock, how you been? Sorry to hear about your friend *Freddy* breaking his arms," he said with a grin.

"His name is Eddie and thanks," I replied.

What a jerk!

-18-

The next two weeks were regular weeks. Our hometown Panthers collected two easy playoff victories, punching their ticket to the state championship in Dallas on Sunday at 7:00 p.m.

Kids at school were fanatical about Polk's playing in the state championship. Everyone was talking about going to AT&T Stadium. I was thrilled; it seemed like the success of the football team helped me forget about the pain of my bass fishing season.

In fact, I had almost forgotten this weekend was the one when Eddie and I were supposed to compete for our own state championship on Lake Somerville.

Almost...

When I got home from school, I saw a unique,

8½ x 11 manila envelope on the kitchen table. Once I saw the address, I knew what it was for.

The Texas High School Bass Fishing Association had its home office in Austin. I knew what the letter meant. It was a cruel reminder of the success I should be having. I took the envelope and threw it in my backpack without opening it.

"I should just rip it up and toss it in the garbage," I told myself.   But I didn't. For some strange reason, I just couldn't.

A part of me wanted to look through the information to see all the cool happenings associated with the big event. I even thought about showing Eddie at the tailgate party on Friday just so he could see all the cool things we had qualified for.

I went to my bedroom and played some video games to take my mind off this weekend. I was playing but quickly got bored. I started scrolling through my social media account, and most of it was about the football game on Friday.

Then I saw something that caught my attention. My eyes quickly squinted, and I had to read it twice. The *Polk County Advertiser*, our local newspaper, had posted an emerging news article titled "Star Panther Players in Big Trouble after Prank."

I clicked on it and couldn't believe what I was reading. In the article, it cited five important starters from the team had gotten in trouble the night before. By law, they couldn't post their names because they were minors. But it did say they were key players.

Some of the players apparently drove up to College Station High School, the team we were playing in the state championship. They spray painted PANTHERS in big, red letters across the front of the school. The next morning the principal watched the school's security camera tape, and the students were quickly identified. The article ended by saying the school was exploring discipline options with the students.

I couldn't help but wonder who would be stupid enough to do this five days before the biggest game in Polk history.

The next day school was much quieter. News of

the prank gone wrong had traveled fast, and everyone was nervous that it could affect Polk's winning the game.

Maybe it was five players who didn't play much. But the article did say they were key players.

Eddie was the first to catch me in the hall.

"Did you hear about the spray-painting incident at College Station?" he asked.

"Of course. I hope it doesn't turn into a big deal. We got a state championship to win," I said.

"Turn into a big deal? You don't know?"

"Don't know what?" I quickly asked.

"Tell me, what do you think our chances of beating College Station?"

"I would say we're the clear favorites, but it should be a really tough game," I said, wondering why he had asked.

"What do you think our chances of winning would be without Desmond Ward?" he asked.

"Zero," I replied and suddenly realized the implications.

-19-

Of all the dumb things Desmond could have done, I figure this was the dumbest. He was one of the players identified on the camera. He had been wearing a clown mask but took it off as he hurried into the getaway car. He has one of the most recognizable faces in all of Texas. It was probably the only time in his life that he regretted people recognizing him.

"Does that mean Des is out for Sunday's game?" I asked.

"I think so," Eddie replied, "but I'm not sure. I know Coach Green and Mr. Bakken have been in the office most of the night and again early this morning trying to figure it out."

"There's no way he'll be able to play on Sunday. Or

is there?" I asked, hoping all the time that it would be true.

"It's Desmond Ward. It's for the state championship," Eddie explained.

He was right. It wasn't fair for all those other players who had worked so hard for a community that supported and cheered on our team all the way to the upcoming state championship. It wasn't like anyone got hurt, but it was still a stupid prank to pull.

Eddie and I went to our first hour biology class when the familiar bell of the PA speaker chimed. It was Mr. Bakken, and everyone could tell that something wasn't right. For the first time that I could remember, Mr. Bakken sounded nervous and unsure of himself.

"Ahhh…good morning, Panther High. Happy Thursday. Today we'll be having chicken nuggets and French fries. Remember to wear your red and black tomorrow to show your Panther Pride! Have a great day!"

We turned and continued on toward our class

when the crackling speaker came back on. "Would Rock Conrad please come to the office immediately. Thank you," he said.

"Did he just say your name?" Eddie asked me.

It all happened so fast I wasn't sure if I heard him right. "I don't think so; he must have said something else." There was no reason Mr. Bakken needed me for anything urgent.

We went down the hallway towards our biology lab. The hallways were empty, and we were about to be tardy. I didn't think Mr. Hill, our biology teacher, would mind, considering we had stopped to listen to Mr. Bakken's announcement.

The bell rang as we walked into class. The entire class sat quietly as Mr. Hill turned towards us.

"Rock, what are you doing?" he asked.

"Mr. Hill, the only reason we're late is because of the announcement."

"Rock, the announcement—that's why you need to go the office. Mr. Bakken asked specifically for you in the announcement," he said sharply.

———

Eddie had heard the announcement correctly. Why in the world would Mr. Bakken need to see me? He had to know I had nothing to do with the spray-painting incident in College Station.

I turned and walked back out of the biology lab while Eddie and the entire class stared at me.

I was on my own.

-20-

My mind raced as I slowly headed towards the main office. I had never been in Mr. Bakken's office before, but I knew it was somewhere in the main office. My mind wandered as I walked.

What could he possibly want with me? Maybe it had something to do with Student Council. I was the treasurer. Yeah, maybe that was it, I thought.

As I entered the office, I was greeted with smiles and head nods from the secretaries. "Are you Rock Conrad?" the first lady asked.

"Yes. Yes, ma'am, I am," I replied.

"Go right back, son, Mr. Bakken is waiting for you," she said, pointing to a large office behind her. Walking in, I saw Mr. Bakken sitting behind a big oak desk. His office was filled with Panther football memorabilia, including football helmets and old jerseys hanging on the wall. My eyes were fixed on Mr. Bakken the entire time. I didn't notice there were two other chairs with people sitting in them.

"Well, hello, Rock," he greeted me. "Thank you for swinging in."

Now I got super nervous. *Why is he being so nice?* He pointed behind me.

"I assume you know Coach Green and Desmond Ward," he said. I turned to see both of them sitting in the chairs. The coach had a hopeful, apologetic look on his face, but Des didn't make eye contact with me. He just sat with his head down, looking at the floor.

"Yeah, I know who they are," I said.

"Good, that's a great start," said Mr. Bakken, breathing a sigh of relief.

"Can I ask why I was called in?"

"I will get to that, young man," said Mr. Bakken. "I have some great news for you. First, we really want you to known how proud we are of you for making the bass fishing state championship at Lake Somerville this weekend. That's quite an accomplishment!"

"Oh, thanks, but I'm not going." I tried to sound casual.

"Well, I had heard something like that, and that's why you're here. I really hope, I mean we really hope that you would reconsider your decision," he said.

I was confused. *We? Who is he talking about, and why do they finally care about bass fishing?*

"Sir, I don't mean to be rude. But I'm confused," I said.

"Well, Rock, I'm going to be upfront with you. We need you to fish in this weekend's tournament."

"Okay, but I don't have a partner," I said.

"Oh, but you do," said the coach, sitting directly behind me.

Did they forget about Eddie's current situation?

I turned back to Mr. Bakken with a confused look on my face. "Who's my new partner?" I asked.

Mr. Bakken just looked at me with an awkward, shrewd grin.

———

"Hey, Rock," said Des, lacking any enthusiasm.

Is this some cruel joke? Why in the world do they want Desmond Ward to be my bass fishing partner this weekend? He had the biggest game of his life ahead of him on Sunday. Plus, he had just gotten in trouble. None of this made any sense.

"Well, it's decided then. I'll take care of the registration for tomorrow," said Mr. Bakken.

"Do I have a choice in this decision?" I asked.

"Not really," Mr. Bakken replied. "But good luck and make Polk High proud!

———

-21-

My mind wandered as I walked back towards class. *Why now? Why this weekend?*

When I walked into the biology lab, the whole class cheered. This was like something out of a weird sci-fi movie. I sat down by Eddie, and he looked happy too.

"You're a celebrity now!" Eddie said with a big grin.

"Eddie, what's going on? All I know is Mr. Bakken is making me fish with Des this weekend at Lake Somerville."

"You really don't know?" he whispered with a surprised look on his face.

"Know what?"

Eddie went on to explain it was all over social media. Mr. Bakken had found a loophole in the school policy and a way to punish Des without his missing the state championship game on Sunday. The athletic handbook stated that Des had to sit out one school event as punishment.

With the big game on Sunday, the only other sporting event that Des was eligible to play in the meantime was the bass fishing event with me at Lake Somerville. If he sat out and didn't fish on Saturday, then he fished with me on Sunday, he would meet the requirements of sitting out one event and be eligible to play Sunday night. So we would be a scratch on Saturday and then fish on Sunday, giving us a slim chance to win since we would miss the first day.

"So they're using me to make sure Des can play after he did something stupid the other night?" I asked as anger stirred up inside me.

"Exactly!" Eddie said.

"I'm not doing it; see how they like that. They can scratch us for both days," I blurted out.

"Dude, you can't do that," Eddie cautioned me. "The whole town and school are counting on you.

Think about it—you'll be a hero. Let him fish with you for one day. You get a chance to go and see all the cool stuff and help our team possibly win a state championship. It's a win-win situation for you. You will be the second most popular kid in Polk High!"

Eddie was right. I wasn't worried about being cool and popular, but I did want to help our football team. I had always loved the game and wanted us to win our first state championship.

The way I looked at it, I had only one choice. I couldn't tell Mr. Bakken no. The school and the whole town would shun me and never talk to me again. I couldn't be the reason we lost to College Station.

If the worse thing I had to do was take Des fishing on Sunday, then I could do it. I didn't even know if Des knew how to fish on that level, but it didn't really matter. We didn't have a chance of winning the bass championship anyway. But the football game…now that was winnable, and I finally had a way to help.

I guess I have a new fishing partner—the one and only Desmond Ward.

-22-

As soon as classes ended, my cell phone started going crazy with texts and messages from other kids at Polk. They were all pretty excited that a way had been found for Des to play. To be honest, I was too. A part of me was glad I could help in a small way for the Panthers. I could put up with Des for one day.

I was bummed we couldn't fish on Saturday, the first day of the tournament. The fishing rules required both partners to fish. That was the way to make the punishment fulfill the handbook requirements allowing Des to play. He had to sit out one event, so he joined the bass fishing team.

Now more than ever, I realized how important it was to have caught the one fish at the G.C.R. event.

Later that night, I received a strange text from a number I didn't recognize. "Thanks, buddy, I appreciate it," was all that it said.

I didn't know who it was until the same number sent me a picture of him holding a huge largemouth bass. So it turned out that Des liked to bass fish.

Now that I knew who it was, I decided to reply.

"Glad I could help. I hope you'll be ready to fish on Sunday," I said.

"Oh, yeah, I love to fish, but just to let you know, I have to leave at 1:00 p.m. at the latest to make it back to catch the bus to Dallas," he warned me.

What? 1:00 p.m.? The official weigh-in wasn't until 1:30, but I wasn't worried about that. There was probably no way we had a chance to win.

"Works for me. I'll pick you up at 6:00 in the morning. Be ready," I said.

"But 6:00 am is early, bro," complained Des.

"Then make it 6:01 a.m.," I replied with a grin.

"That'll work," he said reluctantly.

I walked around school on Friday and felt like a

rock star! Everyone, including teachers, were high-fiving me and smiling at me. Students were yelling out, "We love you, Rock!" "You the man, Rock!" all day.

I didn't hate it; honestly, it felt kind of nice.

Then at the end of the day came Mr. Bakken's Friday announcement.

"It's finally here, the chance for your Polk Panthers to win the State Championship!" Mr. Bakken began. "The game starts at 7:00 at AT&T Stadium. Doors open at 5:30, and the tickets can be purchased online or in the office. Also, we want to give a huge shout-out to our two proud Panthers competing in the state bass championship on Sunday. Good luck, Rock and Desmond. Hope the fish are biting!" Mr. Bakken exclaimed.

Wow, I finally made the Friday shout-outs.

-23-

I spent all day Saturday in my room checking weigh-in results from Lake Somerville. They were catching some decent fish. A part of me wished I was there. I thought about driving there, but it was a long drive, and I couldn't fish. So I didn't feel like torturing myself.

At this event, only the top three fish of the weekend are kept. Those are what counted towards the overall team score.

A lot of eight- to ten-pound bass were caught. The ones who were in the top five caught some hogs. I checked one more time at 6:00 to see who was on the leader board. The last weigh-in was at 5:00, so the day's final results were in. Sitting atop the leader board were the Jones brothers. They had an amazing day on the water with a combined three fish score of 37 pounds.

Even if they didn't catch another fish, there was a chance that those numbers would still hold out on Sunday. It would be tough to beat a 12-pound average.

The second-place team weigh-in total was around 34 pounds, so there was a lot of ground to make up if anyone wanted to beat the Joneses.

However, what made this tournament so exciting was the final weigh-in. Any team could catch three giants on Sunday and move up the leader board, but it was going to be a tough road. I had never caught three fish over 12 pounds on one day, and I had fished some great spots.

Sunday morning, I was up at 4:00, checking the weather. I was so excited; I couldn't fall back asleep. The weather was going to be hot with little-to-no wind, a perfect day for fishing and football.

I had loaded the boat the night before and ended up pulling into Des's house about ten minutes early.

I was surprised he was up and ready. He jogged out to my truck and got in.

"I'm ready, Rock," he said.

He could tell I was a little shocked.

"Make no mistake, I'm a football player, but I love to bass fish too," he said.

At first we didn't say much. But it's amazing the conversations that can happen when two people are driving together in a car. When we finally started talking, he talked about bass fishing, and I rambled on about football.

It was kind of ironic that we were each interested in what the other excelled in. He knew far more than I thought he would about fishing. He even talked about what lures we would be using and the different water temperatures.

When the conversation turned to football, he was shocked with how much I knew. He couldn't believe that I knew how to break a cover two or isolate a wide receiver versus man-to-man coverage. He was also embarrassed about the spray-painting incident.

Turns out, Des didn't do any of the spray painting. He was there, though. He had given into peer pressure and made a mistake.

We were close to Lake Somerville when I pulled off at a gas station to fill up the boat.

"Nice boat," said a grizzled voice from behind me.

I turned to see this older man with a long gray beard who reminded me of Santa Claus at first. Des had grabbed some water and snacks and then returned to the truck. Both of us were standing near the pump when the old man approached my boat.

It was odd; the old man knew we were going to fish Lake Somerville. For the next ten minutes, he told us about something he called the "Bass Factory" where bass as big as our cooler were just waiting to be caught. The catch was that the place was right where alligators lurked.

I wasn't sure how to take the old man at first. *Was he crazy, nosey, or just trying to help?*

Once he started talking about the nearby gators, I wrote him off as crazy. He went on for another couple of minutes before we thanked him for the information and headed out.

I had fished lots of lakes in Texas that had alligators. I avoided them, and they avoided me. I wanted to keep it that way. Plus, I had a hard time thinking any fish would live anywhere near a gator. It just wasn't likely.

Glancing over at Des, I noticed he had a crazy look on his face.

"Rock, I think we need to find that Bass Factory!" he blurted out.

-24-

We pulled into the campground at Lake Somerville where the event was being held. The place was packed, and campers were everywhere. The campground covered 168 acres with over 93 sites, and every one of them had been filled. Sponsor banners were everywhere. This tournament was a big deal.

Lake Somerville itself was huge, with over 11,630 acres of excellent fishing. In June 1962, the U.S. Army Corps of Engineers had set out to create a giant man-made lake. The lake eventually was stocked with a wide variety of fish like crappie, catfish, and largemouth bass. A couple of years ago, Dad had brought me to Lake Somerville, so I had fished the lake one time. We had caught a ton of fish and had a lot of fun.

Big arrows and signs pointed to check-in. When I pulled up, an official-looking judge walked over to my window. "Name and school, please."

As soon as he spoke those words, my heart dropped. I had never submitted the paperwork needed. The packet I was to mail in was still sitting in my backpack in my bedroom back home.

"To be honest, sir, I think I forgot to mail the packet in," I said.

"Well, that's a big problem," he said and frowned.

"We're from Polk High School, and my name is Rock Conrad."

He looked down and took his time scanning the list. "Oh, I see your name here. Did you not fish yesterday?" he asked.

"No, sir. We had to scratch." I hoped he wouldn't hold that against us.

The man cocked his head. "Looks like someone turned in your paperwork for you."

Right. I had forgotten that the principal had said he was going to take care of that.

"And I take it you are Eddie Owens," he asked, looking closely at Des. "Wait…are you Desmond Ward?" the judge asked with his eyebrows raised.

"Yeah. Yeah, I am," Des replied.

"Wow…the man himself! But you aren't listed on the entry form." The judge frowned.

"Yeah, I know my partner had a medical issue, so Des is filling in to help me out," I offered.

"Well, this is unusual, but I guess it's okay as long as one of you are registered. Don't you have a state championship football game tonight?" the man asked Des.

"I sure do," Des responded with a smile.

"Well, good luck fishing and then tonight."

"Thanks, but I was wondering if you could help us," Des began. "My friend here is afraid of alligators. Are there any spots we should avoid today on the lake?"

Des was one smart guy, after all. He knew just how to get information without arousing anyone's suspicions.

"There aren't a ton of gators," the judge replied, "but everyone knows they love to sun themselves on the western side of the lake, directly off Bell's Island. You don't need to worry, though, there are no bass over there anyway. The gators have eaten them all. You two are all set; pull into dock 3 to unload."

Des and I switched spots, and he backed the boat up as I climbed in to prep it for launch. I was surprised at how well Des handled the maneuver. Within minutes I had pushed off, and he left to park the truck. I got the boat tied up next to the dock and was turning on the electronics when I heard a familiar voice.

"Hey, Fish face, what are you doing here?" Jeff Jones demanded.

I looked up at him and glared.

"You know the competition started yesterday, right? Looks like you're a day late and a dollar short," Jack mocked, and both brothers roared.

"Do you two have a problem with my fishing partner?" boomed Des' voice behind them. He had parked the truck and was ready to get on board.

"Yeah, as a matter of fact, we do," Jeff scoffed as the twins turned around towards the voice.

Both boys were shocked to see Desmond Ward standing there. It was actually funny to watch their faces go pale.

I couldn't tell if they were going to wet themselves or ask for an autograph. They just stood there and stared at the 6'5" superstar quarterback.

"We're...we're sorry," Jeff stammered.

"It's not me you need to apologize to," Des declared.

Both boys quickly looked at me. "We're very sorry," both boys cried out in unison.

"This better never happen again," warned Des as both boys scrambled around him towards the end of the dock.

I had a pretty good idea that the Jones brothers weren't going to be a problem anymore.

-25-

"Thanks, man," I said.

"Don't mention it. I don't like bullies," he said. After I told him Jeff and Jack were the first-place team, Des made his plea again about finding the Bass Factory.

"Rock, we need to go to Bell's Island; the judge said all the gators lived there," Des insisted.

"I don't know, I've never caught any big large-mouth anywhere near any gators—ever!" I groaned.

"What do we have to lose? If we find the Bass Factory, we win the tournament. If we don't, we spent a nice day on the water fishing," said Des.

"Have you ever fished near alligators?" I croaked. Somehow my voice went up a notch at the thought of it.

"No, but there is a first time for everything, Rock." He reassured me with a slap on the back.

Suddenly we were committed to Des's plan of following the old man's advice.

I plotted Bell's Island into the GPS, and we took off. We arrived at the spot right at sunrise, and I idled the motor and dropped anchor. The sun just peeked through the clouds, painting the sky a rich orange and purple color. The scenery was nothing short of a masterpiece.

"Isn't God's handiwork amazing?" Des asked, looking around in awe at the beauty that surrounded us.

"It sure is," I replied as we both stared out on lake.

My trance was broken with a big splash off the stern of the boat.

I turned to Des, "Dude, you got to be more gentle with the spinner than that."

"That wasn't me, I haven't even cast yet," Des answered as he showed me his empty hands.

I squinted through the morning haze towards the banks of the islands. I could make out several large trees partially submerged and sticking out of the water. Suddenly one of the trees moved.

"I think we're in the right spot," I whispered, turning towards Des.

"What makes you say that?" he asked.

Gators were everywhere. I wasn't surprised that no boats were anywhere near us. No one was crazy enough to fish here.

I pictured the Jones brothers laughing uncontrollably if they found out we were fishing here. The spot was littered with logs, making almost every cast a snag. Plus, it was loaded with huge gators that probably liked to catch largemouth bass as much as I did.

The old man was probably laughing too. We were the only two guys crazy enough to take his story seriously and fish with the gators. But at this point, it was our only chance of catching huge largemouth bass. I just didn't want any of the gators to mess with Des' throwing arm, not before the big game tonight.

My first cast was perfect, landing right between some big logs. I worked the topwater bait until it got snagged on a bunch of branches that I hadn't seen.

First cast and I had to cut my line. I was already one lure down.

Good start...

-26-

The morning sun added a magical look to Lake Somerville. All of the stress and anxiety I had been feeling about Eddie's accident and the Jones brothers seemed to melt away.

The truth was, I was enjoying my fishing partner's company. We talked and laughed. He wasn't the ego-infested maniac I thought he had become.

But fishing was difficult here. Alligators swirled around us, and partially sunken trees were a hazard everywhere. Each time I thought I had a hit, it turned out to be some hidden snag.

After a half hour, I started to doubt our decision. "Maybe we should pull up our lines and try a different spot," I suggested.

"Rock, do you want to win? Do you want to finally shut up those goofy Jones brothers?"

"Of course I do, but we have a limited time to fish, and this spot has too many hazards. It's just too hard to fish here," I complained.

"Great risks, great rewards, Rock," Des reminded me in his best deep voice.

"We have no chance of winning; we need three fish that equal around a 15-pound average. It's impossible!" I was so discouraged.

"Nothing is impossible, so change your attitude. We just needed to find the Bass Factory, and we did. Quit whining and start fishing," he demanded.

I was shocked at how determined and focused Des was. I knew he was only out here because he had to be, so he would be eligible for tonight's football game. But he wasn't acting like that. He had become a fishing maniac—just what I so desperately needed in a partner!

With newfound determination, I flipped my bait caster, landing my Rooster Tail lure inches from a giant alligator.

The lazy gator paid it no attention as the Rooster Tail weaved through the water. Suddenly, BAM! I felt a massive hit and jerked the rod back, hooking the fish. I bobbed and reeled and fought the fish. It was big, real big. My reel screeched as the fish tried to take out more line.

Luckily, I was ready and hurried to the bow of the boat. As the fish got closer, I could see Des' reflection in the water. He had the net ready. He was quick and exact, swooping up the big largemouth.

He looked at me and grinned. "That old man was right, Rock. We found ourselves the Bass Factory!" he proudly exclaimed.

After landing the fish, we took our portable scale and weighed it.

"Is that right?" I gasped.

"Yep, 14.5 pounds. What a brute! Fish one down; now we just need two more."

I looked at my watch, it was only an hour after sunrise, and we already had gotten a huge lunker.

When I reminded him that we had about three

hours to catch two more, Des nodded and went back to fishing.

After an hour of no bites, our small talk turned back to football.

"I think you guys should be ready for the blitz tonight," I suggested. "College Station is known for their nickel blitzing packages. Keep your eye on #51 Harp—that linebacker is a beast and has a good nose for the job."

Des stopped reeling and gave me this strange look.

"Just because I don't play doesn't mean I don't love football," I explained.

I could tell Des was impressed.

He started talking about the offensive game plan, and I was into it. Then the Bass Factory produced our second fish.

This time it was Des' turn.

-27-

Another big one…

While we hadn't had many bites, when we did get one, the fish were big.

Des smiled and rocked back and forth, fighting the largemouth. He was skilled, maneuvering the fish through a small pile of oak branches. The fish made a run, trying to get the line tangled in the mess and free the lure.

Des was ready. He countered and moved to the front of the boat. This time I netted his fish. It was a nice one, but not quite as big as our first bass. It weighed in at 12.3 pounds—definitely a keeper.

"That makes two!" said Des with a confident look on his face. He really believed that we were going to win the state championship, and he had believed it the entire day. It had never even crossed my mind until now…

"Rock, we just need one more fish over 13 pounds, and we're in!" he announced.

I looked at my watch. We had one hour before we needed to go. Des had to leave at one, but we both had to be present for the weigh-in to count. If we didn't make it back to the docks in time, it wouldn't matter what we caught.

Our talk went back to football and the state championship game tonight.

"Rock, you should be a coach someday. It's crazy how much you know about reading defenses," Des said, shaking his head. He added, "You got any good fourth-down plays?"

"I do. I have a play I call the Maggot that I perfected and use on my video games that works every time." I took out some lures and put them down on the deck to demonstrate the football players and the formation.

"Okay, you start in a tight formation then shift

into a spread look. You sneak the tight end to the right of the quarterback tight to the lineman. Two wide receivers split out to the left and to the right. There's one running back in the backfield. The running back runs in motion to the right towards the single receiver side. The safety will run him. The quarterback fakes a pass to his right, and the tight end slips up the middle of the field wide open."

I looked at Des to see if he agreed.

"That's brilliant!" Des responded. We spent another ten minutes examining the play.

He added, "Man, that's good stuff! I wish I'd have known about this play before today."

I glanced at my watch. It was 12:10, and we had two fish and only about 20 minutes left before we had to make the long trek back to the docks. It didn't look like we were going to reach our three fish limit, but we had a great day fishing at the Bass Factory.

Then I felt a massive hit, and the water exploded around my lure. I set the hook, knowing the fish was big.

My eyes met with Des. He had such a look of confidence. It was like he almost convinced the fish to bite my lure so we could win.

Then there was a second splash, and this time it wasn't the fish.

It was a giant gator.

-28-

My line went slack as I reeled. The alligator had easily cut my fishing line and gobbled up the large bass.

"What were the chances of that gator's getting hungry at the worst possible time?" I said to Des.

Five minutes left. I didn't even have time to put a new lure on. I wasn't upset; we had given it our best.

I started cleaning up and getting the boat ready to head back to the marina. The last thing I wanted was to be the reason Des didn't make the bus for the big game.

I started the engine when I noticed the tip of Des's pole flex. At first, I thought it was another snag.

"Wait one second, Rock," he cried out.

He slowly lowered his rod and jerked back to set the hook. Fish on! He reeled and put tension on his rod. He had hooked a largemouth.

I looked at my watch, and it was 12:35 now. I knew we were going to be pushing the time now.

We still had a 20-minute ride back to the clock, and Des had to drive away at 1:00 in his dad's car.

Des worked the pole to perfection and quickly pulled in the fish. I had the net and scale ready.

The fish weighed in at 13.3 pounds.

"We won; we did it!" Des yelled.

"Des, it's 12:50." I sighed.

Des lowered his head. He knew that he could not be late for the bus. He was already technically on probation from the spray-painting incident.

"What are we going to do?" Des asked.

"Hold on!"

With that, I hit the accelerator and roared back to the docks. There wasn't time to talk as we motored back towards the weigh station. The wind was howling, and even if we had wanted to talk, we wouldn't have been able to hear each other. We pulled into the dock at 1:15 p.m. Des had to leave immediately if he had any chance of making the bus.

"I can't leave you—not now. We're going to win this. You deserve it," said Des.

"Des, we don't have time because both of us need to be at the weigh-in for our fish to count," I reminded him. It would have taken another ten minutes to get the boat docked and fish weighed in. If Des stayed, there would be no way he could make the bus.

"It's not right. I have to stay," Des insisted.

"Des, this isn't about you or me; this is about Polk. The whole town believes in you, and you're going to go out tonight and win our first state championship." I wasn't going to let him miss that.

This time I was the one who was confident.

"It's all good, man; I had a great day," I consoled him.

Des nodded and took off running towards his dad's car waiting in the parking lot.

The main judge walked over and looked in our live well.

"Wow! What a day! You must have found a hotspot. Let's get those fish to the weigh-in," he said.

"We sure did. Sorry but we aren't going to weigh our fish in," I replied.

I took two of the bigger largemouths and walked down to the water and released them. Then I walked back and grabbed the last one, letting it go as well.

The judge stood watching me, dumbfounded.

I didn't need a trophy or a state championship; I already felt like a winner. I walked up and got in my truck. I asked for help loading the boat from two other kids who were standing around.

Within ten minutes, I was in my truck, heading back to Polk. For the first time in a long time, I was happy.

I had to get ready for a football game.

-29-

I could tell that Des felt genuinely bad for me. That was nice, but I knew I was okay with everything. I got a text when I got home that he had barely made the bus and thanked me for a great day on the lake.

My stomach was starting to knot up as I got dressed for the game. There was a lot of pressure on Des and the rest of the Panthers.

I picked up Eddie, and we chatted about the tournament. I told him about the Bass Factory and the huge largemouth we caught. He got quiet and started searching his phone.

After a couple of minutes, he cried out, "Dude… you would have beaten the Jones brothers by three ounces!"

I smiled. I didn't need to hear anything else. In my mind, we beat the Jones brothers when Des approached them on the deck and dramatically changed the way they looked at us.

"I figured," I said.

"I can't believe you aren't going crazy. You don't even seem mad," Eddie said.

Strangely, I wasn't mad.

"I learned more today than I have on a bass boat in a long time. I'm good with everything; trust me," I reassured him.

Fishing with an old friend, finding the Bass Factory, and knowing that I could do it was all the reward I needed.

We pulled into the AT&T Stadium parking lot at 6:00— an hour before kickoff. It was full of Polk Panther fans. We made our way over to Eddie's dad's tailgate, and Mr. Bakken ran towards me.

"Boy, Rock, I can't thank you enough for taking Des fishing today," he said, furiously shaking my hand.

It was the first time that Mr. Bakken ever looked happy to talk to me about fishing.

"How did you guys do?" he asked.

"We both went home winners," I replied with a satisfied grin.

Eddie and I enjoyed the tailgate festivities and ate some unreal food. It seemed like everything tasted better today. I had Texas barbecue on many occasions, but today, everything just tasted better.

After stuffing our faces with the amazing food, we entered the stadium, the home of the NFL's Dallas Cowboys. It was gigantic, and everything was supersized. The video screen was bigger than anything I had ever seen before. I couldn't help but wonder what it would look like watching some bass fishing action on it.

We made our way to our seats directly behind the Polk bench in a crowd of red and black. Panther pride was in full effect, and we were all hoping to make history.

-30-

Looking over the football field, I knew we would have our hands full with College Station.

Their stud linebacker, Harp, was easy to spot. He looked like a grown man who should be playing pro on Sunday. Des was big, but this guy dwarfed him.

We won the coin toss and deferred to the second half, meaning we would start on defense.

We kicked off, and I watched as the College Station Cardinals marched right down the field on our defense and scored in the first minute.

I looked at Eddie. "This is going to be a tough one," I said, shaking my head.

"We'll be fine. Remember we have Desmond Ward!" Eddie shot back.

The pressure on Des had to be overwhelming. Tens of thousands of fans—an entire town—were watching his every move.

While we were fishing, I had asked him why in the world did he go with those guys to spray paint the high school at College Station. His answer was simple and surprising.

"I was stupid; I couldn't tell them no. I didn't want them to think I was a wimp. I just did not want to disappoint them," he said. He always wanted to be the hero.

Today was his chance to be that hero for Polk High. Desmond Ward played the game of his life. Every time the Cardinals would score, Des would make an incredible play or throw a touchdown. Heading into the fourth quarter, both teams were deadlocked at 28-28.

College Station ran a trick play called a Flea Flicker and scored from 60 yards out with 50 seconds remaining. The Cardinals missed the extra point, making the game 34-28 in favor of the Cardinals.

Des would have to drive the football all the way down the field to score. Like a surgeon, he dissected the opposing defense and led the Panthers down the field to the 20-yard line.

Coach Green called his second timeout, leaving Polk with only one remaining. I could see Coach going over play options with his offensive players on the sideline.

The Panthers took the field and ran an out-and-up play to the outside receiver. Jim Johnson #6 jumped up at the goal line as the ball glanced off the tip of his fingers. No touchdown!

Now only one second remained on the clock, giving Des one more chance at history—one play for all of eternity. Coach Green called his final time out.

While the players huddled around, the television crew panned the fans. For some reason, the camera stopped on our section. Eddie and I looked gigantic on the big screen.

Des looked over at the screen at the same time. As soon as he saw me, he smiled and ran over to his head coach. I could see the coach drawing something on the big whiteboard.

Des looked confident as he jogged out for the final play of his Polk career. The Panthers started off in a tight bunch formation. They suddenly shifted to a spread formation, and the running back went in motion towards the single wideout on the right side.

Calmly Des dropped back and faked to the running back and found Jeff Collins, our tight end, wide open in the end zone for the game-winning touchdown. Game over! The Polk High Panthers were state champions!

I couldn't believe my eyes. They ran Maggot, my play!

Chaos followed, and Polk was never the same. It was the most amazing day of my life!

-31-

Four months later, I was lying on the couch, getting ready to clean my truck when the doorbell rang. It was a UPS driver who had a package with my name on it.

I opened it and stood in awe. Sitting in a fancy red velvet box was a gigantic state championship ring. One side had a football on it, and on the opposite side was a largemouth bass.

A note was attached that read:

I think you have a good start to your coaching career. You're the only person I know to win two state championships in one day!

–Desmond Ward

About the Author

LANE WALKER is an award-winning author, speaker and educator. His book collection, Hometown Hunters, won a Bronze Medal at the Moonbeam Awards for Best Kids Series. In the fall of 2020, Lane launched another series called The Fishing Chronicles. Lane is an accomplished outdoor writer in the state of Michigan. He has been writing for the past 20 years and has over 250 articles professionally published. Walker has a real passion for outdoor recruitment and getting kids excited about reading. He is a former fifth grade teacher and elementary school principal. Currently, he is a Director/Principal at a technical center in Michigan. Walker is married with four, amazing children.

Find out more about the author at www.lanewalker.com.